MUSTANG
MACY

HANLEY KIDS SERIES: BOOK 1

DANA WILKERSON

Dana Wil

Mustang Macy
Copyright © 2017 Dana Wilkerson
Cover design by Megan Weitzel

Published by A Novel Companion LLC
St. Louis, MO
anovelcompanion.com

First Edition: November 2017

ISBN: 978-1-948148-00-9

Dedicated to Maura, Claire,
Nicholas, and Vera

May you always be inspired to
live well and serve others

WEDNESDAY
August 2

Dear Miss W,

My name is Macy Isabella Rivera, and you met me today for the very first time ever. You also met Matthew, though you weren't introduced. Matthew is my bike.

Why does my bike have a name? Well, why not? And you're probably wondering why I named him Matthew. He's actually named after a character from my absolute favorite book: *Anne of Green Gables.*

You've seen my bike, so you know he's old and a little worn down, kind of like Matthew Cuthbert, and he's also very dependable. And he's a boys' bike, so it just makes sense that he'd be a boy.

(By the way, why are boys' bikes different than girls' bikes? Why aren't all bikes the same?)

I'm glad you're going to be my teacher this year. I thought I was going to be in Mrs. Fisher's fifth grade class, but she had to move away this summer. When I heard that, I wondered if Miss Berry was going to have to teach the entire fifth grade. But my mom said she was pretty sure the school district wouldn't do that. Instead, they hired you!

You're probably wondering why I'm writing to you. (Well, actually you probably aren't, since I don't plan to ever send this letter to you, so you don't even know I'm writing this.)

Anyway, I'm writing this letter because I just have so many words inside me that need to get out, but all of my talking drives my mom crazy. She says it gives her a headache. I don't think that's really true, and I don't *always* talk, even though she thinks I do.

My three-year-old sister Kinzie, though? She really doesn't stop talking. It's enough to drive a girl up a wall and across the ceiling, especially because we share a room, and there's nowhere to get away from her.

We also share our room with our brother Tanner, who's about to start third grade. He's pretty quiet, though. But that might be because between Kinzie and me, he can't squeeze any words in.

So I met you today, and you seemed super nice, and I think we're going to get along really well. Somehow you just seem like you're someone who's easy to talk to.

And I think I won't drive you crazy, like some of the other teachers I've had. When I was in third grade, Mrs. Statler and I did *not* get along very well at all. But I got through it.

In all of my eleven years I've learned that not everybody likes each other, but you just gotta try to be kind anyway and spend your time with people who like you and who you like back.

I think it's kind of a good thing that not everybody wants to be friends, though. I mean, if we all wanted to be friends with the exact same people, that wouldn't work out too well, would it? There would be a lot of jealousy and fighting, and I don't like fighting.

My mom and my fourteen-year-old sister Kayla fight a *lot*. When that happens I just go to my room, shut the door, and try to disappear into a book.

Kayla is going to be a freshman this year, but she thinks she's an adult. She is *so* not, but when I say that to her, she yells at me and stomps around. Mom says that's just the way girls act when they're fourteen. I sure hope I don't.

As for my mom, when I told her I had met you and you're going to be my teacher, she said she has known you for her entire life, because you both grew up here.

It's been a long time since you've lived in Hanley, though, so I'm going to tell you what Mom is like now.

She might be a little bit different than when you knew her.

First off, she has long blonde hair. She once told me she had short hair when she was in high school, so it's not the same as it was the last time you saw her.

My brother and sisters and I all have brown hair, just like our dad. But Mom and all four of us kids have green eyes. Mom says it's because her family came from Ireland a long time ago. If that's true, I wish I had gotten red hair from them, just like Anne Shirley (of Green Gables). Of course, she didn't like her red hair, but I love it.

Sometimes my mom has a job, and sometimes she doesn't. With four kids and no husband, it's hard for her. She wants to work, but a lot of times she'll get a job, and then one of us will get sick and she has to stay home. Or sometimes the car breaks down and we don't have the money to fix it, so she can't go to work. And then they fire her.

That's not really fair, because what else is she supposed to do? Leave her sick kids home by ourselves? Walk ten miles to a job in Millard? It's not like there's any public buses in Hanley.

I know a lot of people think my mom is lazy, because I've heard them talking when they think I'm not listening. But it's not true. Even when she doesn't have a real job, she does odd jobs for people around town to make money when she can.

Mom tries her best, but she gets discouraged really easily. I try to help her, but there's only so much an eleven-year-old kid can do.

Speaking of Millard, Granny Staley lives there. You might know her, because she used to live in Hanley. I used to be able to see her all the time. But a few years ago Granny's uncle died and left her a house in Millard, so she moved there. Now she only comes over a couple times a month. I'm glad we get to see each other at least that much, though.

I never get to see my dad anymore. His name is Luis, and he and Mom got divorced right after Kinzie was born. He doesn't send Mom as much money as he's supposed to (when he sends her any at all). That stinks because we could really use the cash.

Actually, you probably know my dad, because he went to high school in Hanley too.

Dad lives in Miami, which is also where his parents live. I haven't seen them since I was really little, so I don't really miss them because I don't know them. But I miss my dad a lot.

He used to take me to the park to play basketball. He wasn't very good, but at least he wanted to play with me. Mom won't even try. She says she was always so terrible at basketball in school that the other kids made fun of her, so she never wants to touch a basketball again. I'm glad you weren't one of those kids that made fun of her. Mom said you were always really nice to her.

Okay, my hand is starting to cramp, and it's time for Kinzie to go to sleep, so I need to turn out the light.

Good night, Miss W. I hope to see you again soon!

Your new student,
Macy Rivera

FRIDAY
August 4

Dear Miss W,

Mom told me your first name is Jessica. I like that name. I don't think I've ever known anybody named Jessica before.

I do know people with the last name of Washburn, though. When I met you, we talked about how I know your dad from church. But I know your dad's wife isn't your mom, because they just got married a couple years ago.

Another reason I know she's not your mom is because I know who your mom is. She goes to our church too. You look a lot like her, even though your hair is blonde and hers is auburn. I'm pretty sure she dyes hers, though, because it used to be light brown.

You didn't say if you're married or not, but I am using the deductive reasoning skills I learned in fourth grade to conclude that you're not. Here's how I figured it out:

A) Miss Berry called you Miss Washburn, not Mrs. Washburn or even Ms. Washburn, which I've learned can go either way—married or not married.

B) Your dad's last name is also Washburn. I know some women don't change their last name when they get married, but they're usually famous or something. I'm pretty sure you're not famous or you wouldn't be teaching school in a tiny town.

So my conclusion is that you're not married.

And I also think you don't have any kids, or I would have heard your parents talk about their grandkids. Old people really love to brag about their grandchildren, you know.

My granny even tells me stories about her other grandkids, and I don't really need to know what my cousins are up to, because I usually already know. And they're really not as interesting as Granny thinks they are.

But I do know your sister, Miss Brandi, is about to have her first baby. Miss Brandi is always really nice to me. I see her at church and at the clinic where she's a nurse when I have to go see Dr. Matt.

Speaking of Dr. Matt, he's Olivia Price's dad. Have you met Olivia yet?

She's going to be in our class, and I'm not too happy about that. I wish she was going to be in Miss Berry's class instead.

Olivia is one of those people who doesn't like me, and I don't like her back. We actually used to be best friends. But then right after school started last year, she stopped hanging out with me all of a sudden, and she started acting like she's better than me.

Sure, she's richer than I am. But that doesn't take much. She wears fancy new clothes, while I just wear things the neighbors give me and hand-me-downs from Kayla.

Kayla and I like completely opposite styles, though. She's into trendy stuff, while I'm more comfortable in jeans or leggings and a T-shirt. We can't exactly afford new clothes, though, like Olivia's family can since her dad's a doctor.

I once heard someone say, "The clothes don't make the man." I think that applies to kids too. Olivia might look nice, but that doesn't mean much when she doesn't act nice.

But like with Mrs. Statler, I try to be kind to Olivia even if it's hard to get along with her. My mom always says, "Be kind, Macy. You just never know what other people are going through." I can't imagine what Olivia might be going through that's so bad she has to be so annoying all the time. But I try to be kind even when I don't think she deserves it.

I can't wait until school starts. It's twenty more days, which seems like *forever*. I adore school. A lot of kids don't, but I'm not one of them.

I love to learn new things, and I could read all day long, and my family will tell you that one of my favorite things to do is to talk to people about what I learn.

During the summer I go to the library almost every day to use the computers and Internet, since we don't have a computer at home. And I check out and read two or three books a week—both non-fiction and fiction.

The problem is there's nobody to talk to about all the things I learn and the stories I read. Well, there are people, like my mom and my sisters and brother, but they get tired of listening to me.

Tanner doesn't like to read as much as I do. But I think reading is really important if you want to be successful in life. So this summer I told him that for every book he reads (a chapter book—not a picture book) I'll spend a half hour playing superheroes with him. I already wish I hadn't made that deal with him, because I am *so* tired of superheroes.

But I'm really glad he's been reading more. Even though he won't admit it, I can tell he's started liking to read.

Kinzie, on the other hand, loves reading. Well, she loves to have Mom or me read to her, because she can't read yet. But she thinks she can read, because she has us read the same books to her over and over so many times that she memorizes them.

Every time we go to the library, Kinzie checks out ten books, which is the most the library allows her to get at one time. I think she'd take home a hundred if they would let her.

My mom likes to read too. She goes with us to the library once a week. When it's nice outside we walk there. We usually take the wagon with us so we don't have to carry all of Kinzie's books.

Mom likes to read romance novels, which I think is silly. But she enjoys them, and who am I to tell people what kind of books they should read?

Do you like to read, Miss W? I'm going to say yes, because I think teachers mostly do. I wonder what your favorite book was when you were my age. My mom's was *Little Women*. I like that one okay, but I like the *Anne of Green Gables* books so much better.

Speaking of books, Kinzie keeps asking me to read to her before she goes to bed, so I'll let you go now.

I hope I see you again soon!

Your student,
Macy

SUNDAY
August 6

Dear Miss W,

I heard someone mention your name after church today. I couldn't help but interrupt them and tell them you're going to be my teacher. I know it's rude to interrupt, but sometimes I just can't control myself.

Anyway, this person said she's glad you're coming back to Hanley. I actually heard lots of people talking about you at lunch. I think a lot of people are excited you're moving back here, especially your dad and Miss Brandi.

We always have a potluck lunch at church after the service, and it's amazing. The old ladies fix such good food—like fried chicken and lasagna and baked potato casserole—and they always send some home with me.

I always feel a little weird taking it. But to be completely honest, it's the best food we get all week.

My mom doesn't like to cook, and sometimes there isn't enough money to buy food for every meal anyway. I can handle going without a full meal here or there, but I don't want Tanner and Kinzie to be hungry.

So it's great to get the food from church, especially during the summer when we don't get food at school. The yummy church food lasts for a few days, and then sometimes I do some chores for Mr. and Mrs. Monroe from church to make some extra money.

The Monroes are old and can't do everything they used to. So they'll ask me to plant flowers or wash their car or rake leaves or whatever they need done.

They pay me, and then sometimes they also give me food or books or something else they think I might want or need. I help them, and they help me. It's a pretty great deal.

In Sunday school today, Olivia was acting like a spoiled brat. I know that sounds mean, and I wouldn't say it out loud (except maybe to her), but it's true!

She was bragging about her family's vacation to California and how amazing it was. They went to the beach and to Disneyland and they were even in the audience for a game show. The show will be on TV in December, and I just know she'll talk about it every day until then. It also sounds like she got an entire new wardrobe—like she needs one.

Sure, I might be a little jealous (maybe a lot jealous), because I've never even left Missouri. But Olivia knows that, so she shouldn't have gone on and on about every tiny little detail of where they went and what she bought and what it cost.

That wasn't very kind, and we were even learning about kindness in our Sunday school lesson. She obviously was not paying attention.

I guess the one good thing about her vacation is that I didn't have to see her for three weeks. It was a nice break. I had almost forgotten how annoying she could be. But now I remember all too clearly. Ugh. I wish she would move away.

But enough about Olivia, because there's another person I've had to deal with today who annoys me like crazy.

When we got home from church, Kayla's boyfriend, Logan, was here. And he's still here. I'm not a fan. He's rude to my mom, and he's not always nice to Kayla, and he drives a massive truck that you can hear from about a mile away.

When he comes over, Kinzie and I hole up in our room. But Tanner sometimes talks to him about cars, and every once in awhile they even play video games together. That irritates Kayla, though, because it means Logan isn't paying attention to her.

So it's really best when he doesn't come around. But I can't stop him from coming over. I've just learned to deal with it the best way I know how, which is to avoid him at all costs.

Kinzie's getting tired of playing in our room, though, so I told her I'd take her to the park if Mom says it's okay. I think Mom might go with us, too. I heard her bedroom door close a while ago, so I have a feeling she is avoiding Logan too.

I'll talk to you later, Miss W.

Your student,
Macy

FRIDAY
August 18

Dear Miss W,

You're moving into your house right now!

This morning I went for a ride on Matthew before it got too hot out. When I rode by Mr. and Mrs. Dannon's old house, I saw your aunt Gloria outside.

She and your dad look *exactly* alike, except one of them is a woman and one is a man, obviously. I wonder if they're twins.

By the way, Miss Gloria is one of my most favorite people on the entire planet. She was my Sunday school teacher when I was in preschool, and now she's Kinzie's teacher. She always does fun stuff, and she always talks to me, even though it's been a long time since I was in her class.

Anyway, Miss Gloria waved at me, so I stopped and asked her what she was doing. She was busy getting everything ready for you to move in. Sadly, she said it wouldn't be for a couple of hours.

I was bummed I would miss seeing you. I had told Mom I'd be home before noon so I could watch Kinzie and Tanner. She needed to go clean somebody's house while their usual person is on vacation.

Miss Gloria took me on a tour of your house, though, which was fun. It was empty, of course, except for a bed in the guest room.

The colors you picked out for the walls are great. I wish I could paint the walls in my room, but they're made out of that fake wood stuff, and it's hard to paint. Plus, paint isn't cheap. But if I could pick out a color, I'd choose the green you used in your living room.

Your aunt told me she and your dad grew up in the house where you're going to live. Before I could think about the fact that it might be rude to say it, I told her that it must be a really old house.

She laughed, though, so I don't think she cared. But I still shouldn't have been rude, even though from what I've seen, Miss Gloria doesn't get upset very easily.

I try to not get offended by what other people say, either. Most of the time I know people don't mean to say rude things. They just let the words slip out before they can think about how they might make the other person feel, like I did today (and, let's be honest, like

I do more often than I should). But some people do it on purpose (like Olivia!), which is a whole different story.

Miss Gloria told me some stories about when you were a little girl. I bet it wasn't too fun when you broke your leg on Christmas day when you were six. Or when you rode your bike into a fence while you were learning to ride and fell off right onto your face. Ouch.

While she was telling me about the stories you used to write about a squirrel family in the backyard, Coach Carlyle came to help move your stuff in. He laughed so hard at Miss Gloria's story he was actually crying.

I was so surprised when Coach Carlyle didn't call her Miss Gloria, or even just Gloria, but *Aunt* Gloria! I thought that meant he must be your cousin. But he explained that his uncle was married to Miss Gloria, which means you and he aren't actually cousins. You're just "almost related." I also discovered that his brother is married to Miss Berry's sister. So I guess that means they're almost related too.

Sometimes it seems like everybody in this town is almost related to a lot of other people. I was talking to Mom about it when I got home, and she says that happens in small towns a lot.

Since Coach Carlyle is the high school girls' basketball coach, that means someday he'll probably be my coach. I asked if he thinks the team will win districts this year. He thinks they have a chance, because there are a couple of freshmen that are really good. I told him that when I'm in high school Hanley will definitely win districts, and maybe even state. He said he couldn't wait.

When I got home, Kinzie and Tanner were playing a video game, so I decided to write to you while they're busy doing that. Once they're done I won't get a moment's peace until Mom gets back home.

Speaking of which, they just started yelling at each other, so I'd better go referee.

I'll see you soon, Miss W. I hope you're at church on Sunday.

Your student,
Macy

SUNDAY
August 20

Dear Miss W,

I am absolutely positive this is going to be the best school year ever. Why? Because I have the best teacher ever!

This morning when I got up, it was really cloudy outside. I was hoping the rain wouldn't start before we got to church. It looked like it could start pouring any minute, but Kinzie, Tanner, and I decided to risk it and just hope we didn't get soaked on the way.

Tanner and I usually ride our bikes when we need to get somewhere. But Kinzie's too small to ride a bike, so we have to walk when she wants to go out with us.

It takes us about fifteen minutes to walk to church, and we usually sing songs or play some kind of game to keep Kinzie entertained. (And let me tell you, it can be exhausting trying to keep her entertained!)

Today we played the game where you make up a story one sentence at a time. I would say a sentence, and then Tanner would say one, and then Kinzie would take a turn. Sometimes what Kinzie says doesn't make any sense in the story, but I think that just makes things more interesting.

This morning's story was about a polar bear that floated on an iceberg until it melted off the coast of Hawaii. Then she swam to shore and became a performer at a luau and ate Cheetos all day. (That last part was Kinzie's. She would eat Cheetos for every meal if Mom would let her.)

Kinzie laughed so hard at the story that I thought she was going to puke up her breakfast all over the sidewalk. Thankfully she didn't. Imagine us having to clean that up. Gross.

We got to church and went to Sunday school, and then we went in to the church service. We always sit on the left side, four rows from the front. Dr. Barnes and her husband sit at the other end of our pew.

As you know, Dr. Barnes isn't the kind of doctor that takes care of you when you're sick. I didn't used to know there was another kind, but there is. Mom says lots of people are doctors that aren't the medical kind. People with all types of jobs can go to school for a long time and then be called a doctor. Who knew?

Dr. Barnes used to be a teacher, and now she's our superintendent. She's a little bit scary, but I want to be like her when I grow up.

Yes, I realize that might sound strange, but she is super successful, and someday I want to be a success and make a difference in people's lives. I don't think you can be a teacher and superintendent and not make a huge difference in lots of kids' lives.

Mrs. Lewis used to sit in front of us, but she died this week. She was very, very old, so it wasn't all that surprising. But it was sad. She was always really nice to Tanner, Kinzie, and me, and she'd sneak candy over the pew to us every week.

I don't think Dr. Barnes liked that very much. She would pucker her lips when we took the candy like Mom does when she sees something she doesn't like. But she never said anything. I guess even a superintendent wouldn't tell a really old lady what to do.

Anyway, you came in with Miss Gloria. The service started about two seconds later, so I didn't get to talk to you right then, even though I wanted to. But I hoped you would stay for lunch. And you did! You even got to meet Tanner and Kinzie, and they really liked you.

I wanted to talk to you some more, but there weren't any empty seats at your table. So instead, I just hung around and tried to avoid Olivia. But the church isn't that big, and we ended up at the dessert table at the same time. I know, I know, I should have just walked away, but I didn't.

Olivia was wearing this pink-and-yellow polka-dot dress, and her blonde hair was all curled, and she was prancing around like she was Shirley Temple or something. (My mom likes to watch old black-and-white movies. That's how I know who Shirley Temple is.)

She looked at me and said, "Your dress is *so* 2010."

So I said, "At least I don't look like a prissy little girl," and then I stuck my tongue out at her.

I was sorry as soon as I'd done it, but then she smirked at me like she knew I was sorry, and then I wasn't sorry anymore. Ugh! She makes me so angry sometimes!

Finally everyone started to leave, and Miss Susan gave me a paper bag full of leftovers. I gathered up Kinzie and Tanner, and we headed down the street. And then it started to pour down rain.

Usually, if it's raining when we leave church, somebody offers to drive us home. But this time we were already halfway down the block when it started. And I really, really wished we had waited two more minutes to leave.

Then, like an angel in disguise, there you were in your tiny car, telling us to hop in. It was obvious you weren't too excited about the mud we were tracking into your brand new car, but you didn't say anything.

And oh, Miss W, I can't tell you how happy it made me when I found out that you love *Anne of Green Gables* as much as I do—and not just the first book, but the whole series.

Anne is kind of my hero. She was super smart, she didn't let anybody push her around, and even though she had a terrible childhood before she met Matthew and Marilla, she was able to make something of herself. And you know, I think she would have made something of herself even if she'd never gone to Green Gables, but I'm so glad she found a family.

As I've already mentioned, being successful is very important to me. My mom always says, "Macy, I want you to make something of yourself. You're smart, and if you try hard enough, you can do anything you want. Don't let anybody stop you."

And I won't—let anybody stop me, that is. Someday I'm going to do big things and change the world.

I gotta tell you that even though I was glad for the ride home, I was a little embarrassed to have you see our house. A rundown trailer with broken steps in an ugly trailer park is nothing to brag about. I'm glad we have a home, because I know some people don't. But it would be great if the roof didn't leak when it rains and if I didn't have to share my room with both Tanner and Kinzie.

Someday I'll have a nice house, though. And I'll make sure my mom and sisters and brother have a good place to live too.

Hey, thanks for offering to pick us up for church whenever it's raining. Sometimes Mom will drive us, but she likes to sleep late on Sundays, so she doesn't always get up in time.

Good night, Miss W. I can't wait for school to start on Thursday. I'll see you Tuesday night for "Meet the Teacher," even though I've already met you.

Love,
Macy

MONDAY
August 21

Dear Miss W,

I thought I wasn't going to see you again until "Meet the Teacher" night, but I saw you tonight at Mrs. Lewis's funeral visitation.

I've never been to an actual funeral before, but I go to visitations a lot because it seems like old people at church are always dying, and I like to go tell their families I'm sorry.

When Olivia and I were friends, she always told me how strange it is that I actually like going to the funeral home. I guess maybe it is odd, but I like to talk, and that's what happens at the funeral home—lots of talking and even usually some laughing.

I like to tell funny stories about the people who died. It makes people not so sad for a little while, and I think that's a good thing.

Mom went to the funeral home with me, but we left Tanner and Kinzie at home with Kayla. She wasn't happy about staying at home to babysit, but she decided it was better than going to a funeral home. She doesn't share my love of the place.

I thought it was weird that Mom wanted to go, because I didn't realize she even knew Mrs. Lewis. But Mom said Mrs. Lewis used to come to our house to talk to her sometimes when none of us kids were home. She didn't say what they talked about—just that Mrs. Lewis was a really kind lady. But then I already knew that.

Jacob Wilson's grandpa owns the funeral home in Hanley. A lot of funeral homes look like houses, but they're not. However, Wilsons' Funeral Home is actually a house, and Jacob's grandparents live on the second floor.

Some people think that's really creepy, but I think it's kind of cool. I mean, how many people can say, "I live in a funeral home"? The looks on people's faces would be priceless. It would be a great conversation starter, and we all know how much I love a good conversation.

You got to meet Jacob, who's going to be in our class. He's probably my best friend. We've known each other almost all our lives, because we were on the same T-ball team when we were little. But then after T-ball, they split us up into boys playing baseball and girls playing softball, which wasn't any fun at all.

After Dad left, I stopped playing softball. Mom said we didn't have enough money to pay for my uniform and buy snacks for the team when it was our turn.

It was a bummer, but it's okay. I like basketball better anyway. That's the sport I'm going to play at school when I'm old enough. You don't have to pay money to be in sports at school, so I won't have any problem with that.

I also saw Olivia at the funeral home. Did you see her? Well, she wan't nice, as usual. She said it was ridiculous how Jacob and I act like we're boyfriend and girlfriend.

Ugh. I mean, Jacob is great and all, but he is *not* my boyfriend. And we definitely don't act like it, or at least I don't think so.

You know what I think, though? I'm pretty sure Olivia likes Jacob, and she wants to be his girlfriend. She's always flipping her hair when she's around him and saying silly stuff like girls do when they like boys.

I guess Jacob is cute, and he *is* the tallest kid in our class. But I like him because he's nice and he's smart, and he doesn't act like he's better than I am. And there's *no way* he would ever want Olivia to be his girlfriend. So she can just give up on that idea.

Mom tells me I shouldn't have a boyfriend until I'm much older anyway. She says they're a distraction, and I need to focus on getting good grades and being successful in life instead. I think that sounds like a good plan.

Well, I'd better go because I have to get up early in the morning. I saw Mr. and Mrs. Monroe at the funeral home, and they asked if I could come weed their flower garden tomorrow. It's supposed to be super hot, so I decided to get up early and do it while it's still a little bit cool outside.

Good night, Miss W! I'll see you again tomorrow.

Love,
Macy

TUESDAY
August 22

Dear Miss W,

Tonight was crazy! I can't believe everything that happened. There's so much to say, so I'm just going to start at the beginning.

Mom, Tanner, and I were getting ready for "Meet the Teacher" when mom's stomach started to hurt. That happens to her a lot, and I've noticed it's mostly when she's nervous.

Tonight I think she was worried about having to see Tanner's teacher, Mrs. Statler. They don't get along too well. Mom says they've never really liked each other. So that's probably why she felt sick.

I wish Mom would stand up for herself more than she does, but I can't force her to. On the other hand, I'll stand up for myself any time. I decided that there was no reason for Tanner and me to miss out on the fun of seeing our classrooms and our friends, so we rode our bikes to school.

It's not very far. In fact, it's close enough that the bus won't even pick us up for school, so we're used to getting there on our own.

You already know I love school, but one of my favorite parts is actually walking into the building. On the wall inside the front doors is that massive painting of a mustang.

I love it because it's amazing *and* because my mom painted it. A few years after she graduated from high school, her old art teacher called and asked if she would paint the school mascot. She even got paid for it.

On the other side of the entrance is the trophy case. There are tons of trophies in there for every sport, and there are some pictures too. One of these days hopefully my picture will be in there.

When you go down the hall past the superintendent's office, the walls are covered with the senior pictures of every class that has graduated from Hanley High School. There are too many of them to count. Well, not really, but there are a lot. I like going down outside the high school gym and seeing the one with Mom's picture on it. I guess you're on that one, too.

So last night I dropped Tanner off at Mrs. Statler's room. It was obvious she wasn't happy Mom didn't come, but what could she do? Tanner couldn't go back home without me. He's only eight, and Mom didn't let me start riding my bike around town by myself until I was ten.

Then I backtracked to our classroom, and I could tell you were surprised that Mom didn't come. But your smile told me you didn't mind that I came anyway.

I was pumped to see our classroom. I like the orange walls. They make it extra bright and cheery. And the reading nook is perfect. I can't wait to spend my free time reading in it. The beanbag chairs you put in there look super comfy.

It was a relief to discover that my desk is across the room from Olivia's. She's next to her BFF Zoe. I hate to tell you, but that's a mistake on your part. Those two will cause some trouble unless you split them up.

Zoe just moved here last year, and right after that is when Olivia stopped being my friend and was suddenly BFFs with Zoe. She and I don't exactly get along either. At least she doesn't go to our church, so I get a break from her on the weekends and over the summer, unlike Olivia.

I wish Jacob was sitting by me, but it's probably good that he's not, or I'd be tempted to talk even more than I already do. Instead, I'm between Allegra Starks, who I like a lot, and Rocky Jones. I bet you didn't know that Rocky is named after Barack Obama. He even kind of looks like him.

Anyway, everything was great until Olivia walked in. First, she rolled her eyes at me as soon as she saw me. Then, after she talked to you, she came over and said she couldn't believe they had put us in the same class again, since they know we don't like each other.

I told her that they must know I have the patience of a saint if they thought I'd be able to put up with her for another year.

And then things got worse. A crash came from the hall. We all ran out there to see what had happened, and Tanner was on the ground. A bulletin board had toppled down onto him.

I overheard Mrs. Statler say it was Tanner's fault because he's out of control—he isn't!—but Dr. Matt figured out the board had been loose already, and it could have fallen on anybody.

Dr. Matt was really nice, like he always is. He made sure Tanner was okay, and then he offered to drive us home.

I wasn't too happy about that, because I did *not* want to ride home with Olivia, especially since she was glaring at me. But I didn't want Tanner to have to ride his bike home, because he was kind of shaken up, so I swallowed my pride and let them take us.

We had to put the back seat of their SUV down to get the bikes in, which meant Tanner sat in between me and Olivia in the middle seat. So at least I didn't have to touch her. And I didn't talk to her either.

It wasn't really awkward, though, because Dr. Matt talked to us the whole time. He asked questions about what we like to do and what our favorite movies and books are. He's a really nice man. It's just too bad his daughter isn't more like him.

Mom just told me to turn out the light, so I'd better go. I'll see you in thirty-four hours!

Love,
Macy

THURSDAY
August 24

Dear Miss W,

First off, I know you asked me to call you Miss Washburn instead of Miss W. And I'll try my best to do that when I talk to you, because that's the respectful thing to do. My mom is always telling me to respect my elders, and I try to do it as much as I can. But I'm still going to call you Miss W in these letters, because I like it better and it's shorter.

Now, on to the important stuff. This year I had the best first day of school ever. Sometimes the first day can be a little annoying, because the teacher always asks us to write about what we did over summer break. And I hardly ever get to do anything fun during the summer, like going on vacation or to the water park or whatever.

I mean, I do have fun with Tanner and Kinzie. We play games, and we go to the library, and we love to use our imaginations to pretend we're going on exotic adventures. But that doesn't sound very exciting compared to other kids' stories about actually going to the beach or to Disney World or to the mountains or to visit their uncle in Chicago.

So I was super excited when your assignment was different than usual. When you told us to plan our dream vacation, I knew exactly what to write, because I have often thought about it.

I wrote all of this on my paper today, but I'm going to write it here too because I'm just so elated about it. (Did you see how I used one of our vocab words there? I think I'm going to use "elated" all the time now.)

Dream Vacation to Prince Edward Island
1. Get a passport. (Just imagine all the stamps I'll get in it over the years.)
2. Find somebody with a car who can take Tanner, Kinzie, and me. (Maybe you'll take us, Miss W? Your car is kind of small, though. I'm not sure our suitcases would all fit.) Flying would be fun, because I've never been in a plane. But then I'd miss getting to see all the other things along the way.
3. Plan out the route. Here's the places I want to stop along the way: Chicago, Niagara Falls, New York City, and Boston.

4. Pack my bags.

5. Drive from Missouri to PEI.

6. See Green Gables and all the places Anne went. I also want to: take a buggy ride (they still do that, right?) down the White Way of Delight, have someone row me across the Lake of Shining Waters while I recite "The Lady of Shalott," tell ghost stories in the Haunted Wood, and get drunk on currant wine (just kidding, Miss W).

7. Eat a whole lot of really good food. Maybe I'll hire a personal chef.

8. Spend the rest of the summer just living where Anne lived. Maybe in an old farmhouse. I think it would be magical.

9. Come back home at the end of the summer. (Do I really have to?)

I can't wait for you to read some of the papers aloud tomorrow. I bet Jacob's has something to do with baseball. And Olivia's is probably about going to Europe or being Miss Pre-Teen Missouri or something, both of which she'll probably do, because those are the kinds of things that happen to girls like Olivia.

I'm trying not to be jealous. (Not that I want to be Miss Anything, but I would like to go to Paris. I fell in love with it when I read the *Madeline* books when I was little.)

I'm excited to hear what your dream vacation is, too.

You're probably wondering why I didn't put a star on mine to let you know it was okay to read it to the class. It's because I don't want Olivia to make fun of it, which I'm sure she would do. It's my perfect plan, and I don't want her mean comments to affect my feelings about my dream vacation. It's just for me. And it's for you, Miss W. I know you'll approve.

Tanner and I took the long way home from school today so we could stop by the grocery store and get some candy. Since I made some money pulling weeds for Mr. and Mrs. Monroe the other day, I wanted to give Tanner a first-day-of-school treat.

We both got a candy bar, and we got a roll of sour candy for Kinzie too. She can't get enough of them. Mom says they make her even more energetic than usual, but they make her happy, so I wanted to get them for her.

I also got Mom a piece of her favorite mint chocolate. I was hoping that way she wouldn't be as upset with me as she usually is about Kinzie's candy.

When we got home, Mom was sketching a picture of Kinzie. She's a very talented artist. Our living room walls are literally wallpapered with Mom's artwork. I wish there was someplace in Hanley where she could sell her art, because I know people would want to buy it. It's that good.

I've tried to get her to set up a booth at the spring craft fair at the community center, but she won't ever do it. Maybe I'll do it for her sometime. Mom doesn't have as much "get-up-and-go" as I do. She tells me all the time that she wishes she did, but she just doesn't.

But I think if Mom just had somebody to help push her along, she could do anything she wanted, just like she tells me I can do.

It's been a long day, and it's a school night, so I'd better get to bed.

Love,
Macy

FRIDAY
August 25

Dear Miss W,

Well, I was right about Jacob and Olivia's dream vacations, wasn't I? I'd think it would be exhausting to go to every major league ballpark in one summer, though.

Maybe Jacob should spread that out over a few years. And he might want to think about taking his pal Macy to one or two with him, seeing as how I've never been to any major league games. I haven't even been to one in St. Louis, which isn't very far away.

And I should have known that not only did Olivia want to go to Paris and some other places, but to also go on a shopping spree while she's there.

Bo-ring. Why would you waste your time in Paris shopping when you could be looking at art and going up the Eiffel Tower and cruising down the Seine?

Your plan sounds super fun, though. It's kind of like mine, but bigger, where you'd be going to more than one place where a favorite book is set. Since you want to go to Prince Edward Island, too, you might as well take me along with you.

You have also made me want to read *Pride and Prejudice*. I asked Mom if she's read it. She had to read it in high school and didn't really like it because it was so long and the teacher asked really strange questions.

But she read it again as an adult and really likes it. She has a copy in her room that she said I can borrow if I want, but she doesn't recommend it for a fifth grader. I should probably wait a few years.

She also told me that she has watched the TV miniseries a few times, and I always refused to watch it with her because I couldn't understand the characters' British accents. Plus it's really long. But maybe I'll try again the next time she watches it.

At school today we had art class, and Mrs. Yang put us in pairs to work together on a project. And do you know who she paired me up with? Olivia. Of course. And we argued the whole time.

If I suggested we use paint, she demanded we use colored pencils. If she wanted to use a glue stick, I was sure liquid glue was the best choice. We couldn't agree on anything. Actually, I think we didn't want to agree on anything—at least I didn't. Why should I have to do everything the way she wants to do it?

Thanks for taking time to talk to me after school. It's kind of nice to know that you also had somebody you didn't get along with when you were my age.

Don't get me wrong. It's not great that you didn't get along with her, but it's nice to know I'm not alone. But it's sad that you were once best friends and then all of a sudden you weren't, and you *still* don't get along more than twenty years later.

I think you should forgive her, Miss W, and make up. Maybe you could be best friends again if you were friends before.

But now that I think about it, I might know who you're talking about: Mrs. Statler. I bet I could ask my mom and she'd know, but I think that would be considered gossiping.

I don't like to gossip. I know how it feels to have people talking about you behind your back, and I don't want to do that to other people. I guess I gossip some here in my letters to you, but nobody's ever going to see them, so that makes it okay. I hope.

Anyway, if it *is* Mrs. Statler that you were talking about, maybe you wouldn't be friends now even if you did forgive her. She's really hard to get along with, as I've already mentioned.

You're probably thinking that I should do the same thing—forgive Olivia. And maybe I will someday in the distant future. But I don't really want to forgive her, because she's obviously not sorry when she's mean to me. And I also don't really want to be friends with her again, even if we did forgive each other.

I have a feeling this is going to be a very long weekend. Now that school has started and I'm getting used to going somewhere every day, I'm not sure what I'm going to do tomorrow. I'll probably hang with Kinzie. She's missed me the last two days since I've been back in school.

In fact, she's trying to get me to play with her right now. She's really into memory matching games these days. They're super easy for a fifth grader, but I try to be patient with her and help her remember where the matches are. I even let her win sometimes. Tanner hates it when I do that, but he's not in charge of me, so I can do it if I want to.

Speaking of Tanner, he keeps tossing a little bouncy ball at me to try to get me to play with him. He refuses to stop, even when I yell at him, so I guess I'll end this letter and play with him and Kinzie.

I hope you have a great weekend!

Love,
Macy

WEDNESDAY
August 30

Dear Miss W,

I heard some upsetting news today. I was telling my mom all about you and how great you are and that I hope you're Tanner's teacher and then Kinzie's teacher when they're each in fifth grade.

She told me that she heard you're only planning to be in Hanley for one year. You only came here because you lost your job in St. Louis this summer, and this was the only job available for this school year. Apparently everyone knows you're planning to go back to the city after this year.

Is that true?! Why? Don't you like us? Don't you like Hanley?

Your family all lives here. Miss Brandi is about to have a baby—won't you miss her if you leave? And our class is awesome, even if Olivia is in it. I guess you wouldn't have us in your class again next year, but the fourth graders are awesome too.

I'm just going to have to make sure I do everything I can to make you love it here so much that you don't want to leave. I don't think there's any way I could actually stop any schools in St. Louis from trying to hire you, but I can do my best to make you not want to go back. I'm not sure yet how I'm going to do that, but I'm going to try!

I don't know if I'm going to be able to sleep tonight.

Love,
Macy

MONDAY
September 4

Dear Miss W,

Today is Labor Day, so we didn't have school. I asked my mom why it's called Labor Day, when most people don't actually do any work on this day. But she didn't know, and the library was closed, so I couldn't get on the Internet to find out.

A lot of people spend the day having a barbecue or a family reunion or going to Six Flags. We didn't do any of that, which isn't surprising, because we rarely do any of those things. But I still wanted to have a good holiday and for Kinzie and Tanner to have a good day, so I took them to the park.

We played for a little bit, but by 10:30 it started to get really hot, so we headed back home. We walked by your house on the way, and you were outside weeding your flowerbed.

I was surprised when you invited us to stop and have some popsicles with you. Kinzie loves popsicles, and I was dying to see the inside of your house with all of your stuff in it.

Your house is awesome, Miss W. The lemon yellow walls in the kitchen were just perfection. It made it so cheery in there. And your huge couch with all those green and purple pillows? I wish I had it as my bed. It was that amazing. Not that anything wouldn't be better than my mattress on the floor, but still.

And then you asked if we wanted to stay awhile and play some games. Of course we did.

The amount of games you had was very impressive, since you don't have any kids. But I guess it makes sense because you're a teacher. And I was shocked you have a video game system. I think it's a little crazy that you only got it to do workout games, but that's just me.

It's funny that you like to play Cycle Chase. Tanner loves it too, so I'm glad you had it and wanted to play it with us. I thought you were going to fall on the floor laughing at Kinzie dancing all around the room while trying to get her cycle to go where she wanted it to.

I wasn't much better at the game than she was, though I did mostly stay in one place. But Tanner and you were both really good and very competitive. When you started trash talking, we didn't know what to do, but then Tanner joined in, and you laughed, so I knew it was okay.

It was no surprise that Kinzie wanted to play Memory. Thanks for letting her win. It made her so happy.

Then it was my turn, and even though it was so hot outside, I was hoping you'd say yes when I asked if we could play basketball in your driveway. I don't get to play basketball very often, and it was great to play with someone who's good.

I had never played H-O-R-S-E before, and I was so surprised that I won. I don't think you were even trying to let me win. And then you gave me some tips on shooting layups, which was super helpful.

We learned how to do layups during gym class at school last year. But since there are so many of us in our class, we didn't really learn to do them well.

Plus, I'm left-handed, but we only did them right-handed at school, so that wasn't very fun for me. But you're left-handed, too, so you were a great person to teach me how to do them the right way.

You surprised me again when you offered to share your leftover spaghetti with us. I didn't want to bother you more than we already had, but Kinzie and Tanner were already saying yes, and I wasn't sure if there'd be a whole lot to eat if we went home.

It was really good, Miss W. Thanks!

While we were eating and talking about anything and everything, I was ecstatic to hear that you and Miss Berry are friends. I was hoping you were, because if you have good friends here, maybe that will make you want to stay! I think you two should be BFFs.

Once we finished lunch, it was super duper hot outside, so I was relieved you offered to drive us home.

Then tonight Mom surprised us by telling us she'd watch a movie with us. Usually she just wants to watch romantic comedies or old black-and-white movies, but this time she said she'd watch anything we wanted.

We don't have a whole lot of movies, but we have a few, and us three kids decided on *Cars*. (Kayla was out with Logan, so we didn't have to find a movie she liked too. That's good, because we would never have agreed on *anything* if she had been here.)

Mom doesn't usually get excited about watching kid movies, but I think she actually enjoyed it. She said she'd never watched it all the way through, but it was really a great story.

And now it's way past my bedtime, so I'd better turn off my flashlight and get to sleep. It's a school night, after all! I'll see you tomorrow.

Love,
Macy

FRIDAY
September 8

Dear Miss W,

I was hoping I'd see you at the high school football game tonight, but I don't think you were there. Today at school, Jacob asked if I was going, and I said no. I wanted to go, and I even had the three dollars to get in after helping Mr. and Mrs. Monroe with their garden on Wednesday after school.

But I knew it would be dark after the game, and Mom wouldn't want me to ride my bike home in the dark. And she doesn't drive anywhere unless she has to, because as she says all the time, "Gas doesn't grow on trees!"

When I told Jacob that, he said they would take me home, and they might as well pick me up on the way there too. So I went, and Mr. Wilson even paid for me to get in, which was very nice of him.

I tried to pay for myself, but he said his family has a rule that the oldest person always pays. So since he was the oldest of all of us, he had to pay. I couldn't really argue with that, could I?

The game was *so* much fun. I haven't been to many football games, and we don't watch it on TV at my house, so I didn't know the rules. But Jacob explained them to me as we watched.

Football is an interesting sport, but I don't think I would want to play it. It seems like there's a lot of standing around. I would rather play basketball, where you're constantly moving up and down the court.

It was also fun to see the marching band. Jacob and I went to the very top of the bleachers to watch them. You can see how they're moving around better when you're up high.

They made the shape of an H—for Hanley—which isn't really all that difficult, since it's just three straight lines. But then they marched into the shape of a mustang, which was a lot more complicated and pretty impressive.

I think it would be fun to be in band when I'm in middle school next year. Jacob and I talked about what instruments we'd like to play, but then I told him we can't afford an instrument, so I doubt I'll be able to be in band anyway.

He said if you play the drums, you don't have to buy anything, because the school owns the drums. So maybe I'll play the drums. I can't imagine Mom letting me practice them in the house, though, so that plan might not work.

Granny gave Tanner a harmonica for Christmas last year, and Mom took it away from him after one day because she said it was driving her insane. I'm sure drums would be ten times worse.

Olivia and Zoe were at the game too. They spent the whole time standing along the fence doing the cheers along with the cheerleaders. I hate to admit it, but they were actually pretty good.

Jacob and I walked by them at halftime. I know they saw us, but they just ignored us, which is fine, because I didn't want to talk to them anyway.

It was a close game, but the Mustangs won in the end. Our team has a really good running back. (I just learned what that means tonight.) Jacob told me he's only a sophomore, which means our team should be good for a couple more years just because of him. Jacob says he'll make All-District and maybe even All-State.

Then Jacob told me that the last time somebody at our school was All-State in any sport, it was you, Miss W. He says you're the best basketball player our school has ever had. Wow! Why didn't you tell me that when we were playing at your house the other day? I guess that would be bragging, though, wouldn't it? So I guess it's okay that you didn't tell me. But it's still pretty neat.

Miss Berry was at the game. She was sitting with Coach Carlyle and Mr. Mike, Jacob's uncle. I wonder if Mr. Mike is her boyfriend. I would ask Jacob, but he doesn't like to talk about "girlie things," as he calls them.

I know Coach Carlyle isn't her boyfriend. At least he better not be, because everyone was talking about how he kissed you at the baseball game in St. Louis a couple weeks ago, and it was on the big screen. (By the way, I think that would be super embarrassing. Who wants 40,000 people to see them kissing?)

As you know, that gossip is all over town *and* our classroom. And I am curious about whether he's your boyfriend, but I think it would be weird to ask you, so I won't. But I hope he is, because I think he's really cool, he's a great basketball coach, *and* because if you marry him, then maybe you'll stay here in Hanley.

Well, I'm about to fall asleep, so I'd better go.

Love,
Macy

MONDAY
September 11

Dear Miss W,

I am elated about the community service projects you're having us do! I love helping other people.

When I grow up and become successful, I want to do it by serving others in some way. I think that's more of a sign of success than making a lot of money. Not that I wouldn't like to make a lot of money too, but why not do both, right?

And yes, I know money isn't everything, but when you don't have a lot of it—or even enough of it—you realize it's more important than some people think. I want to have enough money so that I can support my family *and* give a lot away to other people and to charities and stuff.

I'm also excited about learning more about the reformer you told us about: Mercy Otis Warren. I made

Tanner stop by the library with me on the way home so I could get on the Internet and look up everything I could about her.

Tanner wasn't too happy that he had to spend a half hour at the library after spending all day at school. But he got over it when he discovered they had gotten in a few new comic books.

Back to Mercy Otis Warren. You told us that she was a reformer who was involved behind the scenes during the American Revolution and the beginning of the United States. She wrote a lot of papers and essays and letters related to the Revolution and our new government being set up.

I didn't know, until you told us, that back then women really weren't allowed to talk or write about anything important. I think that's absolutely crazy. Why would the world just ignore half of its population?

Anyway, I'm glad she stuck up for herself and for women and told people what she thought, even if some people didn't want to listen to her because she was a woman.

Did you know that she was even friends with President John Adams and his wife? Well, they were friends until Mercy wrote some things about him in some history books that didn't make him look good, and then they apparently weren't friends anymore. Ha!

I like her. I'm glad you told us about her, and I'm glad you want us to be reformers right here in Hanley. Mercy is definitely going to be my inspiration. If I have a daughter someday, maybe I'll name her Mercy. But that could be a little confusing, since it sounds a lot like Macy.

I'm relieved that you put Jacob and me in the same group for these projects. It would have been awful if you had put Olivia and me on the same team. Can you imagine what a disaster that would have been?

So now let's talk about these projects you want us to do. You said they should be solutions to problems we see right here in Hanley. When you asked for ideas of problems, I was so annoyed when Olivia raised her hand, and I was even more annoyed by her response: "We don't have enough clothing stores. Actually, we don't have *any*. That's a *huge* problem. We have to drive *forever* to buy my designer jeans."

Are you kidding me?! She thinks that's a real problem?

She was trying to be funny, but really she was just showing off. At first I was annoyed that you thought it really was an issue for Hanley in a way. But once I thought about it, I realized you were right. We don't have anywhere nearby to buy clothes, and that's not good for families without much money either.

My mom is always complaining about how it costs her ten bucks just for the gas to get to SaveMart and back. We don't have an extra ten dollars lying around, and I know other people who don't either. If there was somewhere to buy cheap clothes right here in Hanley, people would be able to save that gas money.

I liked some of the ideas we came up with for how to solve that problem. I think creating a clothes closet at a church would be a fantastic idea. My cousins in Columbia get most of their clothes free from a church down the street from them. They say some of the used clothes there are gross and old and stained, but a lot of them are perfectly fine, and some of them are even name brands.

But you know what I think? The clothes shouldn't be 100 percent free. That might sound weird, coming from a kid whose family doesn't have much money, but it's partly a matter of pride.

There are a lot of adults like my mom who would like to be able to buy things for their family, but they can't for some reason or another. And they're ashamed when other people give them things.

They usually do take free things because their family needs them, but if they can buy things—even if they're super cheap—they feel better about it. I know my mom does.

See, it's things like this that make me so much different from Olivia. She doesn't even have a clue there are people who can't afford any new clothes, much less designer ones.

And then there's me, who has rarely gotten any new clothes in her eleven years. Even those come from the nice old ladies at church at Christmas.

I can think of a lot of other problems right here in Hanley that we could solve. One of them is that there are a lot of old people who don't know how to use the Internet or their smart phones, but it could be really helpful for them.

They could buy things online so they don't have to drive thirty minutes to SaveMart. Or they could learn things or pay their bills or even see a doctor.

Speaking of which, did you know you can have a doctor's appointment online? Dr. Matt was telling me about it at church yesterday. It's really cool, and it sounds like it's really easy.

It would be great for old people who have a hard time leaving the house or who don't have a way to get to the clinic or who get sick on a Friday night. Because we all know if you get sick on a weekend in Hanley you have to drive fifty miles to get to a doctor. So an online doctor is a great solution to that problem, but if you can't use the Internet, you can't do it.

Anyway, I'm going to keep thinking about problems in Hanley and how I can help solve them. I might even start solving some on my own, outside of what we decide to do in school, because I want to get started doing something right now.

Like I could totally teach Mrs. Monroe how to use the Internet. Her daughter gave her a tablet for her birthday, but she told me she's had a hard time figuring out how to use it.

I think I'll stop by there tomorrow and ask her if she wants me to teach her. I don't know why I didn't think of that before. But at least I've thought of it now, right?

Good night, Miss W!

Love,
Macy

THURSDAY
September 14

Dear Miss W,

This has been a busy week! I did stop by to see Mrs. Monroe after school on Tuesday, and she was over-joyed to have me teach her how to use her tablet and do things on the Internet. She said I could come over once or twice a week to help her.

She tried to pay me, but I wouldn't let her, because I want to do this as a community service project, not a job. (But she is still paying me to help out in the yard and around the house, which is good, because I do need to make *some* money.)

Since I don't have a smartphone or even the Internet at home, you might be wondering how I even know how to use a tablet. Well, my granny has one, and she lets me use it. And really, I think they're pretty easy to figure out once you get the basics down.

First I just showed her the different apps and how they work. Then we downloaded some new ones, like a few games, some news apps, and a social media app.

She told me her friends keep talking about seeing pictures and getting news on social media, and she feels left out. So I helped her make an account, and I even took a picture of her in her flower garden for her profile picture. By the time I left, she had fifteen friends, and she had written a note to someone she went to high school with a hundred years ago.

Hey, I wonder if her picture is on the wall in the high school. I bet it is, because I'm pretty sure she grew up here. I'll ask her when she graduated and then look for her year the next time I'm in that part of the school.

The next day I helped her order some books to be delivered to her grandkids in Texas. While we were doing that, she was telling me how much she loves to read. But she has read everything in the library that she wants to read, and books are so expensive that she doesn't want to buy a lot of them. So I told her she should get an e-reader app.

Since I don't use one, I wasn't exactly sure how it works, but we downloaded it and figured out how to use it together. Then we discovered there are thousands of free books for it, so we downloaded a bunch. She was elated.

You know what? I was excited too. It's fun to help people. I don't get to help people very often except for the ones I live with, and it was a great feeling.

I really like Mrs. Monroe. And I like Mr. Monroe too, even though he's really, really quiet. He mostly just sits in his chair and watches us, which could be creepy, but it's not. I understand that some people just don't like to talk. That's not me, of course, but as my mom says, it takes all kinds.

Then tonight I was back at the Monroe house. Mrs. Monroe is hosting a book club meeting tomorrow, and she needed help cleaning the house.

While I was sweeping the basement (by the way, why did the basement need to be cleaned for a bunch of old ladies to hang out in the living room?), I saw a stack of old games, and one of them was called "Hey Pa! There's a Goat on the Roof." Let me tell you, there was no way I was not going to find out what that game was.

I was tempted to pull it out right then and there, but I figured I should ask Mrs. Monroe first. So I did, and she told me to bring it upstairs and we'd play it. We set it up on the kitchen table, and Mr. Monroe even played with us. He said he used to love playing it with his kids.

It was a pretty silly game, but we had a great time playing it and imagining what the goats were thinking when they were hanging out at different places on the board, like the well or the woodpile. We laughed until we cried. I asked Mrs. Monroe if I could bring Kinzie by sometime to play it because I think she would love it. Of course she said yes.

Next week Mrs. Monroe wants me to help her figure out how to pay some of her bills online. I'm not sure I will know how to do that, so this weekend I'm going to go to the library and see if I can figure it out. I bet Miss Joan can help me.

Do you know Miss Joan? She is ancient and has been the librarian for about a thousand years. Well, maybe not quite that long, but a long time. But even though she's old, she knows everything about computers and the Internet.

Hey, maybe she should run a class to teach other old people to use the Internet. I think I'll mention that to her.

I'll see you at school tomorrow, Miss W.

Love,
Macy

TUESDAY
September 19

Dear Miss W,

I haven't written in awhile, but there hasn't really been much to report. School is good. Jacob and I are trying to figure out what we're going to do for our project. Olivia is still being Olivia. She pretty much just drives me crazy.

Music class is going to be fun this year, because we're learning to play the recorder. Thank goodness the school provides the recorders for us, because otherwise I'd be out of luck. They're not very expensive, but still, as I've mentioned before, there's no way we would have enough extra money to buy one.

Mom often makes me practice it outside, because she gets tired of hearing it, but then the neighbors complain. So sometimes I take my recorder to the park and play it there.

And that makes me think Mom will definitely not let me play the drums next year when I'm in middle school. I mean, if she can't even handle a recorder, she definitely won't put up with drums in the house. Plus, how would I be able to get a drum back and forth to school on Matthew?

Last Saturday I went to the library to ask Miss Joan to show me how to help Mrs. Monroe pay her bills online. She explained how to use the websites for the electric company, the cable company, and the City of Hanley. I never realized how many bills grown-ups have to pay. And Miss Joan says that's not nearly all of them.

I also talked to Miss Joan about having a class at the library for old people, and she thought it was a great idea. She said she'd talk to some of the people who come into the library a lot and see if they would be interested. In fact, there was a man there that heard us talking about it, and he said he would come to a class like that.

Yesterday I showed Mrs. Monroe what Miss Joan taught me, and she was surprised by how easy it was. After I helped her with the first bill, she even figured out how to do the rest of them by herself.

Mrs. Monroe is a really good gardener, and she bought a whole bunch of mums last weekend at a farm outside of town. I helped her plant them today, and she gave me two to take home. She said that I've done such a good job helping with her garden that she thinks I need some flowers at home.

I was going to plant them in the ground outside our trailer, but Mom said she had some old pots somewhere that we could paint and then plant the mums in. She crawled under the trailer to find them, and then we cleaned them up.

We each painted one, planted our flowers, and set them out on our tiny front porch. Hers looks a lot better than mine does, of course, but she said I did a really great job. That's high praise coming from an accomplished artist like her.

Hopefully I'll be able to keep the flowers alive. Kayla thought it was dumb to plant some flowers that are just going to die when winter comes anyway. But I said there was no reason we couldn't enjoy them for a month or two. And maybe we can bring them inside when it gets cold and keep them alive a little bit longer. But if we do, first we are going to check the pots for critters.

One year, Mom had this plant that she kept out on the porch. Then she brought it inside one night when it was supposed to get really cold out. We were sitting around watching TV when all of a sudden a snake head popped out of the pot.

Us girls all screamed and jumped up on the couch when it slithered out. But Tanner wasn't scared. He told us it was just a garter snake, and garter snakes never hurt anybody. Mom didn't care. She just wanted it out of the house.

So Tanner walked over, grabbed that snake by the tail, opened the door, and tossed it out. Even after a few years, just writing about it is giving me goose bumps. Yuck. I don't want a rerun of that experience.

Well, that's about all there is to tell you for today. I'll see you in the morning.

Love,
Macy

SATURDAY
September 23

Dear Miss W,

Today I had my September Mom Date. What's a Mom Date? Well, every month my mom takes each of us kids out to do something—just the two of us.

It's usually something that doesn't cost any money, which is okay by me. I just like spending time with Mom without the others. I mean, I love my brother and sisters (well, it's sometimes debatable whether I love Kayla or not—just kidding!), but sometimes I just want Mom to myself, you know?

Last month she took me to see a movie at the theater in Brayer. Somebody had given her a gift certificate. She wouldn't tell me who, just that it was someone very nice. Now that I think about it, I wonder if it was Mrs. Lewis. She was the type of person who would do something like that.

We saw a movie that's based on one of my favorite books when I was little: *The Worst Vacation Ever.* It was pretty funny, but it didn't really follow the book all the way, which was annoying.

There was no way we could tell Kinzie we had gone to the movie. She would have been absolutely furious. *The Worst Vacation Ever* is currently her favorite book. She's seen the movie previews on TV, and every time they come on, she won't shut up about how she wants to go to the movie theater to see it.

Kinzie has never been to the theater. Mom says she wouldn't be able to sit still long enough for the entire movie, and there's no reason to waste money on a movie nobody will get to finish watching. Kinzie keeps pleading to go, but Mom hasn't given in yet.

So anyway, when we got home, we just told Kinzie we had gone to Brayer and walked around and got some food. We didn't really lie, because we did walk around, and we did share a bag of popcorn at the theater. We just didn't tell her the whole truth. Sometimes you have to do that with little kids, you know?

This month for my Mom Date, Mom didn't tell me what we were doing ahead of time. But she told me to put on my swimsuit under my clothes, so I knew we were going somewhere with water. Today was really hot for September, so I was glad I'd be able to cool off when we got to wherever we were going. We got on the highway and drove past Millard, and then we turned off onto a gravel road. I finally realized where we were going: Mill Bend State Park.

I love Mill Bend. There was an old sawmill there, and part of it is still standing, but you can't go in it because it's too dangerous.

There's a creek that runs by it. (There has to be a creek to turn the wheel on a sawmill, you know.) Up above the mill is a series of waterfalls. Below the mill, the creek widens out and there's a swimming hole with a cliff above it that's great for jumping.

It turns out that Mom had worn her swimsuit too, and the two of us jumped from the cliff over and over again. Sometimes we did it separately, and sometimes we held hands and did it together, which was more fun.

When we got tired of swimming, we walked up to the waterfalls so we could dry off. Mom had me sit on a rock in front of the falls, and she sketched me.

She keeps a sketchpad and pencils in her bag all the time so she can draw whenever she wants to. So she sketched me on the rock with the waterfalls behind me. It was really good. She told me that when we got home she was going to add some color to it.

Mom is working on it now. Well, she's trying to. Kinzie keeps climbing up into her lap, so that's making it kind of hard. Kinzie usually gets really possessive of Mom when she gets home from a Mom Date with one of the rest of us, and sometimes she ignores whichever one of us went on the date. It can be frustrating, but she's little, so I forgive her.

When Mom finishes the sketch, I'm going to put it on the wall over my bed. Then I'll be able to look at it every morning when I wake up and remember how much fun we had today.

Did you and your mom do Mom Dates when you were little, Miss W? I think everybody should do them, but when I've told a few other kids about them, they look at me like I'm crazy. But I tell them they should do it, and they should do dates with their dads too, if they have them, or with their grandparents or their aunts and uncles.

There's a lot of things in my life that I'm sure I'll forget, but I don't think I'll ever forget any of my Mom Dates.

Well, I'd better go try to distract Kinzie so Mom can finish my sketch. I'll see you at church tomorrow.

Love,
Macy

MONDAY
September 25

Dear Miss W,

Today when we were working on our community service projects at school, I was a little bummed that you didn't have time to really talk with Jacob and me. But we're doing just fine on our own. We came up with a ton of things we could do to make our community better.

Jacob was kind of annoyed that I already gave away my idea of teaching the Internet to old people to Miss Joan at the library. But I convinced him that if she's willing to do it, we might as well let her. And then we can do something else, which means even more will get done. Makes sense, right?

But since we were on the topic of old people, that made Jacob think about the nursing home. His mom is a nurse at Hanley Care Center. He heard her talking about how they don't have enough money to keep doing everything they're doing, so they had to fire a couple of workers. One of those people was the lady who did fun things with the old people, like singing and crafts and bingo and stuff.

Jacob's mom was bummed that they wouldn't have activities for the people at the nursing home anymore. She said anything that can help them use their brains and socialize with other people is really good for them. It improves their quality of life. And I'm thinking that since their lives probably aren't very exciting anyway, they really need some fun things to do sometimes.

So Jacob thought maybe we could do some things to help out. We can find volunteers to play music for them so they can sing or dance or just listen if they want. We can ask people to teach them how to do arts and crafts. And we can help organize it and even help lead some of it if it's things we know how to do.

We didn't have time to talk much more about it, but we'll keep thinking about it and get something figured out soon so we can begin planning and then actually start doing it after Christmas.

You told us we need a liaison to assist us in figuring out details, getting things done that we maybe can't do ourselves, and connecting us to the people we need to talk to that can help us out in some way. The good thing about our idea is that we already know an adult who can be our liaison. Jacob's mom said she'd be happy to help out with anything we do at the nursing home. So that part is done.

I overheard you talking with Olivia's group about their project. It seems they're going with the problem of there being no place to buy clothes in Hanley. I have a lot of ideas on that one, as you already know, but I doubt Olivia would want my input. So I'll probably just keep it to myself.

On the way home from school today, I stopped by the library again to ask Miss Joan how plans are going for the Internet class. Five people have already signed up. How cool is that? They're going to start next Tuesday. I'll make sure to stop by after school to see how it went.

Mom's calling me to come help Tanner with his math homework. She says they do math different now than they did when she was a kid. That sounds weird to me. Aren't numbers still numbers? But that's what she says, which means she has trouble helping both of us with math. So I'd better go see what I can do.

Love,
Macy

SUNDAY
October 1

Dear Miss W,

Well, church was interesting today. You know how Pastor Connor has been preaching a lot of sermons on forgiveness? Of course you do, because you're always there, sitting next to me.

I always try to pay attention to the sermon, because I think Pastor Connor usually has some great things to say. And today he really did, and it even made me think that maybe I should forgive Olivia. I knew it was just the right thing to do, even though I didn't necessarily want to do it.

But then, at lunch, Olivia and I got to the dessert table at exactly the same time. (That *always* seems to happen.) There was only one piece of strawberry cheesecake left, and Olivia knows that's my favorite dessert. And she doesn't like it very much—she even picks the berries off! Olivia looked me right in the eye, grabbed a plate, and took that last piece of strawberry cheesecake. Can you believe it?

So what did I do? Well, as she was walking past me with an annoying smile on her face, I "accidentally" bumped into her. She dropped her plate, and cheesecake splattered everywhere. I could tell she was mad, but right then Dr. Barnes came up, so Olivia couldn't say anything to me. Instead, Dr. Barnes helped her clean it up, while I grabbed a brownie and headed back to my table.

I know I shouldn't have acted like that, but she made me so mad! I had been thinking about forgiving her for being such a jerk to me, but then she had to go and make me angry again. No way was I going to forgive her after that.

The worst part was, when I looked up after Olivia dropped her plate, Tanner and Kinzie were watching me. I should have told them that what I did was wrong, because I want to be a good example for them. But instead I just acted like it never happened and started talking to them about what we were going to do that afternoon.

When I got home, though, Mom could tell something was wrong. She asked me if something happened at church. I broke down and told her what I did. She was disappointed in the way I'd acted. She reminded me that she's always telling me to "be the bigger person" and do the right thing, even when other people do the wrong thing.

She said I should apologize, but she wasn't going to force me to do it. I need to make that decision on my own because I choose to, not because I have to.

I'm not sure I choose to yet.

Well, I gotta go. I'll see you tomorrow. Hopefully I won't be quite as mad at Olivia in the morning.

Love,
Macy

TUESDAY
October 3

Dear Miss W,

I'm so elated that Jacob and I have a plan for our community service project. You told us yesterday that we need to decide between providing music or starting an art class at the nursing home. We thought it would be best to ask his mom which one she thought the residents (see? I've stopped calling them old people, like you asked me to) would like better. So last night Jacob talked to her about it.

A church in town just contacted them about doing music once a week, so that means art classes would be perfect for us to do. The room we'd need to use is being used for something else right now, so we won't be able to do it until February. That's perfect, though, because first we need to raise money so we can buy the supplies we need.

The nursing home can't afford to provide the supplies for us, which means we need to come up with the money ourselves. So now we're talking about what we can do to raise the money, and we decided it should be something that is a community service project too. Pretty cool, huh?

I'm also ecstatic because Mom said she'd teach the art classes! Jacob and I will be her helpers, but she'll decide what projects to do, and she'll show everyone how to do it. My mom is such an amazing artist, and I'm glad she'll get to show everyone how talented she is.

Honestly, I was a little surprised she said yes. But she knew how much I wanted her to do it, and she also likes to help people, even though she doesn't get to do it very often. She says usually it's someone else helping her and our family, so it'll be nice to be able to help others in some way.

Isn't it great how our projects are helping us inspire other people to serve the community too? First there was Miss Joan at the library, and now my mom is involved. This whole project thing was a fantastic idea, Miss W. I'm so glad you're having us do it.

When we got home from school today, Mom told us to all hop in the car. She had gotten a check in the mail from my dad, so we were going shopping. I thought she meant we were going to SaveMart, and we did, but we also went to the craft supply store.

Mom hadn't gotten any new art supplies in a long time, so I was glad she was able to buy some new stuff. She can't stop talking about the projects she might do with the residents at the nursing home. Maybe this will motivate her to start making things to sell. We'll see.

Usually when Dad sends money, he also sends letters for each of us kids. This time he just wrote one for all of us together. It wasn't very long, either.

He said he misses us and he hopes he'll be able to come visit us soon. It would be so great to see him, because I miss him too, but I'm not holding my breath. If he can't get enough money together to send to Mom to help feed us, I don't know how he thinks he'll ever have enough to pay for gas or a plane ticket or a bus ticket to come see us all the way from Miami.

It really stinks to have divorced parents. But then I guess you know that, because your parents are divorced too. That's one more thing we have in common, but I wish we didn't.

Sorry to end this on such a depressing note, but that's just the way things go sometimes.

I'll see you tomorrow, Miss W.

Love,
Macy

FRIDAY
October 6

Dear Miss W,

Who was that lady that was with you at the football game tonight? I bet she's one of your friends from St. Louis. And she probably wants you to move back there after this year too. But I don't, and I might have a plan to make you want to stay. More on that later.

Those T-shirts you and Miss Berry were wearing tonight at the game were really, really, really cool. When I'm on the basketball team someday, I'm going to tell everyone we should get shirts just like them, with a girl shooting a basketball from the back of a horse on the front of the shirt and "Mustang Macy" (or whatever the person's name is) on the back. I think "Mustang Macy" sounds really fun.

When I got home, I told my mom about the shirts. She says she actually designed them in art class. That's so cool! She explained that your basketball coach's first name was Sally, and a long time ago there was a song called "Mustang Sally," which is where the idea came from.

Mom thinks Mrs. Monroe probably listened to that song when she was young. (It's so hard to imagine Mrs. Monroe ever being young!) The next time I'm at her house I'm going to show her how to download it onto her tablet.

Jacob and I had a good time at the football game again. Mr. Wilson bought us some cotton candy, which was yummy. And it worked out well, because I like the blue kind better, and Jacob likes the pink better, so we didn't argue over who was going to eat which part.

You know, Jacob and I argue a lot, but it's a different kind of arguing than I do with Olivia. With her it's like we're just trying to make each other mad, and neither of us will give in for any reason. But with Jacob, we're just each giving our opinion, and then we work things out and we compromise if we need to.

During the game Jacob and I came up with a plan for how we're going to raise money for the supplies for our art class at the nursing home. We're going to run a basketball league for fourth and fifth graders.

Right now there aren't any opportunities for elementary kids in Hanley to play basketball like there is for soccer or baseball or softball. So that makes it a community service project because we'll be solving a problem.

It's going to take a *lot* of planning and will involve a lot of people, but we don't care. We both love to play basketball, and we're not afraid of doing big things. We'll play four Saturdays in a row in January. And that will actually solve another problem, because January is always so boring. There's *never* anything to do.

Anyway, there will be four teams, and each team will play the other teams once, with two games on each of the first three weeks. Then on the last week we'll have a championship game. People will pay to watch the games, and we're also going to sell candy. Jacob's dad can buy it at PriceCo, and we'll sell it for a lot more than we pay for it, so we can make a good profit.

One thing we won't do is make any of the kids pay to be on a team. I don't think it's fair when you have to pay to play, because some of us can't afford it.

We'll need referees and coaches and money takers and candy sellers and enough players for four teams. We decided to ask Miss Berry to be a coach and to be our liaison (since she's a teacher and we're doing this at school). Jacob's going to ask his uncle Mike to be a referee, and I'm going to ask you if you'll coach my team! I really hope you'll say yes. I think you'd be a fantastic coach, and I'm also hoping it will make you enjoy living here so you'll stay.

While we were talking about our league, your mom walked by, and Jacob and I decided that we should ask her to coach a team too. We didn't really think she would do it, but we thought it would be cool to have the superintendent as a coach.

So I marched right up to her and asked her, and she said yes! She said she played basketball when she was in high school a long time ago, and she coached your summer league teams when you were in junior high and high school.

Then she offered to buy T-shirts for everyone! I asked her if we could get ones like the one you were wearing tonight. She pointed out that our teams would each have their own mascots, and they wouldn't all be Mustangs, so that probably wouldn't work. She said we could talk more about it some other time.

Dr. Barnes also said she'd check the school calendar to make sure the elementary gym would be available for us to use in January for practices and games. But she was pretty sure it would be because nothing ever happens in January. (See? That's what I said too!)

Before I could head back to Jacob and tell him the great news, Dr. Barnes asked me what happened with Olivia at lunch on Sunday. I didn't want to tell her, because she's the superintendent. I didn't want to get in trouble for it, even though it didn't happen at school. But I also didn't want to lie to her, so I told her what happened.

She said I ought to apologize to Olivia. I responded that Olivia should apologize to me too. She thought I should forgive Olivia whether she apologized or not because I'd feel a lot better if I did.

I'm not sure I would, but I'll think about it. Frankly, I'm kind of tired of hearing about forgiveness from *everybody* these days. I wish I could just forget that Olivia exists instead. Too bad that's not an option.

Okay, I don't want to think about that anymore, so I'm going to bed. It's getting hot here under the covers with my flashlight anyway. Kinzie was whining about the light being on, so I had to hide to finish up.

Good night. I can't wait to tell you all about the basketball league idea in real life!

Love,
Mustang Macy

SUNDAY
October 8

Dear Miss W,

Oh my goodness, there is so much to tell you about. Of course, you know about some of it but not nearly all of it.

First, it was amazing that you and your friend, Miss Dani, picked us up for church in her convertible. I had never ridden in one before. I was really hoping that the rain would stop during church so we could put the top down on the way home, and it did!

When I'm old and successful and have a lot of money like Miss Dani, I'm going to buy a convertible too. Maybe I'll be a lawyer just like her. Lawyers help people, right? Since I want to help people *and* make a lot of money, that might be a good plan.

Second, can you believe that story Pastor Connor told about Mrs. Lewis's husband throwing a chair and accidentally killing their son? Wow! That was so crazy! And it was sad. I wouldn't have wanted to forgive him at all. But it was really cool how Mrs. Lewis's friends convinced her to go to church, and then she learned about how important forgiveness is, and she forgave her husband even though he never asked for it.

And it's really cool that her situation then made her want to help other people who needed to forgive someone. I wish I could have talked to her about it all before she died.

But the whole thing reminded me of what my mom and your mom both said to me this week: that I should forgive Olivia even if she doesn't apologize to me. And I realized I shouldn't just forgive her for what happened last Sunday, but also for everything she has ever done or said that hurt my feelings or made me mad.

So while we were waiting for the ladies to get lunch ready at church, I just went up to her and told her I forgive her for all the mean things she's said and done to me. At first I thought she might smack me, until I asked *her* to forgive *me* for all the things I've said and done to her.

She just looked at me for a minute, but then she admitted it was dumb for us to fight all the time. She said she was sorry for the way she has treated me, and she knew she needed to forgive me too.

So she did. We even shook hands on it.

Then I asked why she started being mean to me in the first place. She said it was because I had been mean to her. I told her that wasn't true. We had been friends, and then all of a sudden we weren't friends, and she was hanging out with Zoe all the time. It turns out Zoe told her that I said she was stupid and ugly, and I was only friends with her because I felt sorry for her. (Can you imagine?!)

I told Olivia I never said any such thing, and at first she didn't believe me. So I asked her when I had ever lied to her. She admitted that I might annoy her in a lot of ways, but she had never known me to lie.

Then I pointed out a couple of times when Zoe had lied at school, which Olivia also knew was true. And then she was mad at Zoe for lying to her. But I told her that she might as well forgive Zoe too, but that didn't necessarily mean she needed to trust her in the future.

So that was huge. And I feel so much better now that I've forgiven her. I think I would have been happy with just forgiving her, but it made it even better that she was sorry for what happened and she forgave me too.

I wonder if we'll be friends again now. I think maybe I want to, since we've forgiven each other. I don't think we'll argue any less, but maybe we can be nice about it and work together like Jacob and I do. And I think I can help her with ideas for her community service project, and maybe she can help us with ours.

Then, while you were busy helping get lunch set out, I decided I needed to have a little chat with Miss Dani. I felt like she needed to understand how much we need you here in Hanley.

I told her about how you're helping the kids in our class do good things in the community. I explained that Miss Berry needs you here to be her friend. And I also told her that I wanted you to still be here to be Tanner and Kinzie's teacher when they're each in fifth grade.

She understood all of that, but she misses you and wants you to come back to St. Louis. But, she pointed out, it's obviously your decision and not hers or mine, so we'll just have to wait and see what you decide to do.

At lunch I told you all about our plan for the basketball league, and I could tell you think it's a pretty big project for a couple of fifth graders. But we're pretty smart kids, and we have a lot of people who are going to help us.

And we're motivated because not only are we doing something that will benefit our community, but it's also something that we're going to enjoy planning and being a part of ourselves. I think that's important when you decide to do something. It just makes sense that if you do something you enjoy and believe in, that makes it a lot easier to do.

I'm so bummed that you might not be able to coach my team, though. I know it's exciting for you that you might be Coach Carlyle's assistant coach at the high school. But it would also be exciting for me and the other fourth and fifth graders if you coached us.

Though now that I think about it, if you and Coach Carlyle would be able to get the team to win districts this year, maybe that would get you so elated that you'd want to stick around another year to see if you can do it again.

But again, that's not my decision, so I'll just have to wait a week to see what you decide. I wish you could do both, but you wouldn't be able to come to our practices if you were coaching the high schoolers.

As if all of that wasn't enough excitement for one day, then you and Miss Dani took us home and *came inside our house.*

You could probably tell I wasn't too happy about that. But Kinzie was determined that you would come in to get the picture she drew of you, so I couldn't really stop you without her throwing an absolute fit.

I didn't want you to come inside because our trailer isn't very nice. Mom always keeps it super clean, but everything is really old, and nothing matches, and

Mom's collection of ceramic owls is kind of weird. And I don't even have a real bed—just a mattress on the floor across from Kinzie and Tanner's bunk beds.

I wish you hadn't seen that, because I don't want you to feel sorry for me. Your house is so much nicer than mine, and I'm sure Miss Dani's is too, since she's a lawyer.

But you and Miss Dani were super nice, and I was proud when she said she was impressed by Mom's artwork. I could tell you were too.

Mom is definitely qualified to teach the art class at the nursing home. I wish she had gone to college so she could teach art at the high school. But she didn't, and I doubt she'll ever be able to even if we had a lot of money, since she has all of us kids to raise.

Kinzie's picture of you was pretty good, wasn't it? I couldn't draw nearly that well when I was her age. Actually, I can barely draw that well now. Art isn't really my thing. I'm more into reading and writing.

One more thing, Miss W. I was absolutely, completely, and overwhelmingly embarrassed by the way Kayla treated you. I wish she had waited five more minutes to come home. I'm so sorry she was mean and rude and tried to kick you out of our house. It's not like she owns it or anything. She had no right to act like she was queen of the castle.

Well, my hand is starting to cramp after writing all of that, and it's way past my bedtime, so I'm signing off.

Love,
Mustang Macy

MONDAY
October 9

Dear Miss W,

Today at school, Olivia and I were actually nice to each other. We didn't hang out at recess or anything, but we were partnered up in gym class to hit volleyballs back and forth, and it was fun.

I thought maybe, just maybe, we could be friends again. We really did have a good time together when we were friends before.

And then after school I was at home doing my homework when somebody knocked on the door. That was a little weird, because nobody ever knocks on our door. They just come on in.

Anyway, I opened the door, and it was Olivia! Her nana was taking her to Burger Hut for dinner, and she asked if I wanted to go with them. My mom said it was okay, so I went.

While we were in the car, Olivia's nana asked me about my group's project at school. I told her all about it. After asking me a ton of questions, she asked Olivia if she was going to play on one of the teams.

Olivia said she might, but what she'd really like to do is lead a cheer squad for the league. She knows a few girls who wouldn't want to play basketball, but they would love to cheer.

I thought that sounded like a pretty good idea, but I told her she had to plan it and be in charge, because Jacob and I already have enough to do. She had no problem with being in charge, which was no surprise. (Now I'm saying that in an "I know my friend" kind of way instead of a sarcastic way.)

We got to Burger Hut and ordered our burgers and tater tots. Olivia's nana sat with Mrs. Daniels, who was in there by herself, so Olivia and I got to sit at our own table.

We were talking about how weird it was to be hanging out again, and then we were talking about forgiveness, and that made me think about you and Mrs. Statler. I know I shouldn't have said anything to Olivia about it, but I did. Sorry.

Anyway, we decided since we had forgiven each other and felt so much better after doing it, you need to do the same with Mrs. Statler. You should forgive her for what she did to you in fifth grade *and* for sometimes being mean to you now.

However, we realized that you probably wouldn't actually be friends again like Olivia and I are. But at least you could get along and not let her bother you anymore, right?

And *then* you came in! We could tell from the start that you were shocked to see us together. Olivia and I looked at each other and grinned, and we silently made a pact not to tell you what happened unless you asked. It didn't take you long.

Telling you what happened between us was also a great way for us to then inform you that we thought you should forgive Mrs. Statler. I thought it was funny that you were surprised we knew who it was that you didn't get along with.

It's pretty obvious when we see you together at school, especially on the playground. When it's you and any other teacher on recess duty, you talk to each other, but when it's Mrs. Statler, the two of you stand on opposite sides of the playground and don't even look at each other.

Everybody knows you two don't like each other. It seems like you're nice to her (at least when us kids are watching), but she's sometimes mean to you even when we're around. That doesn't seem very professional to me.

It's not surprising for Mrs. Statler not to like someone. She doesn't really get along with anybody that I know of. But you're nice to everyone and get along with people really well, except for Mrs. Statler. Anyway, I hope you do forgive her. You'll feel much better afterward. I know this from experience.

Before we left, Mr. Anderson came in. His daughter Grace is a freshman, and she's an excellent basketball player. When she was in junior high, her team never lost a game.

She's also really nice to me and talks to me whenever we see each other. She and Kayla were friends in elementary school, but they're not anymore. Well, it's not so much that they're not friends, but they just don't spend much time together these days.

They didn't have a fight or anything. They just started hanging out with people they had more in common with. Once they were in seventh grade, Grace started playing pretty much every sport. Kayla, on the other hand, doesn't have an athletic bone in her body. So they don't see each other outside of school very much.

It was obvious from the look on your face that you were excited about maybe getting to coach Grace. And that makes me happy for you but sad for me. I have a feeling you're going to choose the high schoolers over us kids. But I'm trying my best to stay optimistic.

It sounds like Mr. Anderson might coach a team in our league, though, which would be cool, because he used to be a great basketball player. So now we have Miss Berry, Dr. Barnes, probably Mr. Anderson, and hopefully you as our coaches.

On the way home from Burger Hut, Olivia's nana was talking about how she has a new smartphone, but she's having trouble figuring it all out. I told her about how I've been helping Mrs. Monroe with her tablet and using the Internet. I said I could help her too, or she could go to the class at the library.

She was happy for the offer, and she invited Olivia and me over to her house for dinner on Thursday so we can help her out. I hope she makes lasagna. She brings that to church sometimes, and it's delicious!

Now I gotta go read Kinzie her book so she can get to bed. It was great to see you tonight, Miss W! I'll see you again in the morning.

Love,
Mustang Macy

TUESDAY
October 10

Dear Miss W,

Today on the way home from school, Tanner and I dropped by to see Mr. and Mrs. Monroe. Mr. Monroe has been in the hospital, so I wanted to check on him. He was doing okay, but he was sleeping right then. Mrs. Monroe said I could come back later and eat dinner if it was okay with Mom.

I told her I thought Mom might be going out with a friend, so I would need to stay home. She said I could bring Tanner and Kinzie along with me if that was the case.

When I got home, Mom's friend was at the house, and they weren't planning on going anywhere, so I didn't need to take Tanner and Kinzie with me. Tanner decided he didn't want to go anyway, and Mom didn't want Kinzie to go with me because she wasn't sure Mr.

Monroe needed a toddler around when he was trying to recover from being in the hospital.

When Kinzie heard that she was missing out on going with me because Mom wouldn't let her, she lost it. She threw such an intense fit that I was actually a little impressed by her commitment to it. Mom, on the other hand, was not impressed.

Mom ignores Kinzie when she throws a fit, because she says Kinzie just wants attention. That worked when Tanner was little, and then he would calm down. But with Kinzie, it just makes her even angrier.

Kinzie was still screaming and pounding her fists and feet on the floor when I hopped onto Matthew and headed out. I felt bad for leaving, since it was kind of my fault that Kinzie threw a fit in the first place. (I should have mentioned the whole thing to Mom while Kinzie wasn't listening.) But I knew it could be a while before she settled down, so I took off.

It turns out that Mr. Monroe was a little disappointed that Kinzie didn't come. He had been hoping to play "Hey Pa! There's a Goat on the Roof" with her.

I won't be telling her that he wanted her to come. That will only make her madder. (Is that a word? Or is it "more mad"? I'll have to ask you tomorrow.)

Anyway, I told the Monroes all about our plans for the art class and basketball league. Mrs. Monroe's face lit up when I mentioned basketball. She's a huge fan and goes to all the high school games. Mr. Monroe goes a lot, too, when he feels up to it. They both said they would come watch me play.

Mr. Monroe even said he'd help sell tickets or candy or whatever I needed. Mrs. Monroe didn't offer, but I think it's because she would rather watch the games than sit out in the hall and sell things. And that's okay, because we need people to watch and then go home and tell other people they should come the next week.

I could tell Mr. Monroe was actually more interested in the art class at the nursing home, because he kept asking me questions about it. I didn't have a whole lot of answers for him, since planning for that is on hold while we do the basketball league.

But I'm pretty sure that when we're ready to get going on it he'll want to help us with that too. His sister lives at the nursing home, and he thinks she'll want to join the class. He showed me a small painting on the wall in their hallway that she painted a long time ago. It was pretty impressive.

We were so busy talking about all of my plans that we lost track of time. Mom called Mrs. Monroe to make sure I was still there and hadn't been kidnapped or anything. It had even gotten dark, so Mrs. Monroe told Mom she'd bring me home.

She drives an absolutely massive car. She's had it forever, but since it still runs, she sees no reason to get a new one. Makes sense to me.

Anyway, the trunk was big enough for Matthew, but you should have seen the two of us hauling him up into it. We finally got it done, but when we got home, Mom had to come out and help us get him back out.

When we got inside, I was still so worked up about our plans that I couldn't stop chattering to Mom and her friend about it. I think they were a little annoyed that I was bothering them, but they also said they were really impressed by our plans for both the nursing home and the basketball league.

Mom offered to run the scoreboard if we still need somebody. She wants to help raise the money for the art class, since she's going to be leading it. And her friend said she would come to the games. Her kids aren't old enough to play, but she has a nephew in fourth grade, and she thought he'd probably want to.

I think this whole thing is going to be a huge success, Miss W! It's going to be a ton of work, but I'm not afraid of hard work. I'm also not afraid of sleep, and it's time for that, so I need to go. I'll see you tomorrow.

Love,
Mustang Macy

THURSDAY
October 12

Dear Miss W,

Tonight was so much fun! Olivia and I went to her nana's house for dinner, like I told you, and we *did* have lasagna. Yum! Then we showed her how to use some apps on her new phone and taught her how to use emojis. She thought they were absolutely hilarious. She kept sending a bunch of them to Olivia's phone. I wish I had a phone so she could text me too.

Then she got a call from her sister in California. She said it would be a while before she could take us home, and we could do whatever we wanted. We went for a walk, and as we were walking down your street, we saw Miss Berry's Explorer and Coach Carlyle's truck in your driveway.

We could smell wood smoke, and it seemed like it was coming from your backyard, so we decided to investigate, just in case your backyard was on fire. It wasn't.

Coach Carlyle was sitting next to a fire pit, and you and Miss Berry were inside. He invited us to stay, so we did. I asked if he thought you were going to coach with him this year. He wasn't sure, but he really hoped so.

I told him about our league and how we wanted you to be one of our coaches. Olivia pointed out that no matter which decision you make, you'll disappoint one of us. (Leave it to her to be Debbie Downer!) I like Coach Carlyle and all, but I really hope he's the one you disappoint. He did say he'd be a referee for our league, though, so that's cool.

You and Miss Berry finally came outside, and you sure were surprised to see us. But Miss Berry was more surprised than you, because she didn't know Olivia and I are friends again.

And then you told us you had forgiven Mrs. Statler! *Whoop!* You have to be so glad you did it. I know it won't be easy to be kind to her when she's not nice to you in the future. But it will build character, as my mom says.

I didn't want to admit this to anyone there tonight, but that was the first time I've ever had a s'more. I've heard kids talk about them, of course, but we've never made them at our house because we don't have a place to build a fire. We don't really have extra money to buy the stuff to make them anyway. Mom's pretty strict about only getting the food we absolutely need and not wasting any money on snacks.

So it was fun to have s'mores tonight. I just watched how the rest of you made them and pretended like I knew what I was doing. I think I did a pretty good job, even though I did get melted marshmallow everywhere. But so did Coach Carlyle, so that made me feel better. And they were so tasty!

I can understand why everybody loves s'mores so much. I really want Tanner and Kinzie to be able to try them sometime too. Maybe I'll suggest we make them for dessert at a church dinner sometime.

As Olivia and I walked back to her nana's house, she asked me if I wanted to come over for a sleepover tomorrow. I was about to say yes when she added that Zoe would be there too.

So then I had to stop and think about it. I'm pretty mad at Zoe for lying to Olivia about me last year. I mean, it made us not be friends for a long time!

Olivia said that she had talked to Zoe about it. Zoe apologized to her and explained that she did it because she was the new kid, and she wanted Olivia to be her best friend. But she knows it was a really mean thing to do to us. She promised that she wouldn't lie to Olivia ever again. Olivia told her she needs to apologize to me too, but she hasn't done it yet.

I decided I'll forgive her even if she doesn't say she's sorry. But I don't really want to spend an entire night with her if she doesn't.

Olivia understood that, but she really hopes Zoe will apologize and I'll decide to come to the sleepover. Mom says I can go to Olivia's if I want, so we'll just have to see how things go with Zoe tomorrow.

I guess we'll also see what you decide to do about coaching tomorrow. I have to admit I'm pretty nervous about that. But there's nothing to do but wait. And I just realized I might actually have to wait until church on Sunday to find out what you choose, because you might not make your decision before school is out tomorrow.

Oh, Miss W, I *really* hope you decide to coach my team!

Love,
Mustang Macy

FRIDAY
October 13

Dear Miss W,

Usually I write about things in the order they happen, but I can't do that this time because I'm so elated. I have to start with the best part.

After I got home from school, someone knocked on the door, which, as I've said before, is strange for us. I knew it was too early for Olivia and Dr. Matt to be picking me up, so I had no clue who it could be. It was you!

In my entire life I have never been so shocked. You explained that you wanted me to be the first to know that you're going to coach my team! *Yippeeeeee!* And you're going to coach the high school girls, too!

I don't know why I didn't think of your solution earlier: be Coach Carlyle's assistant *and* be an assistant coach for Dr. Barnes's team in our league. That way if you have to miss one of our practices, it's not a big deal because there will be another coach. And I think it will be fun that you'll be coaching with your mom. It will be like when we do the art class at the nursing home, and I'll be helping *my* mom.

The other thing that happened today was at morning recess Zoe came up to me and apologized. I forgave her, of course. But I also told her she'd better not lie about me *or* to me ever again. She promised that she wouldn't. She even pinky swore.

I guess that means she and I are friends now. It's kind of weird. Tonight at Olivia's it might be weird, too, but hopefully it will just be fun instead.

So yes, I'm going to the sleepover. I haven't been to a sleepover since Olivia and I were friends before, so I'm kind of excited about it, even with the whole Zoe thing.

Olivia said we're going to make s'mores (yay!) and play her new dance video game and watch a movie in their theater room. Can you imagine having a whole room in your house just to watch movies in? They have recliners in there and everything. And there's a real popcorn maker!

Then we'll all three sleep in Olivia's room, because she has one of those awesome bunk beds that's a double bed on the bottom and a single bed on the top. Olivia's room really is pretty great, even though I hate to admit it because I might be a teeny bit jealous.

She has a chair that hangs from the ceiling (how does it not pull the whole ceiling down?) and a walk-in closet that's almost as big as my bedroom. My closet is minuscule (another vocab word), and I have to share it with two other people.

But when I'm at Olivia's I'll try to be thankful for what I do have and not focus on what she has that I don't. I can't promise I'll succeed. But I'll try.

A car just pulled up, so that's probably Olivia. You made me promise that I wouldn't tell anyone about your decision until seven o'clock, when you will have told your family and friends at the football game. I hope I can keep that promise, but I have a feeling Olivia's going to wonder why I'm so excited and will figure it out whether I say something or not.

Gotta run!

Love,
Mustang Macy

SATURDAY
October 14

Dear Miss W,

I was right—Olivia did figure out that you decided to coach my team before we even got to her house, so I went ahead and told her and Zoe everything. And Dr. Matt heard us talking about it in the backseat, so then he knew it all too. But I made them promise not to tell anyone else until after seven.

Since you've opened up a coaching spot in our league, I asked Dr. Matt if he'd like to help us out. And he said yes. It'll be good to have him around, because if anyone gets hurt, the doctor will already be there.

Also, Jacob saw Mr. Anderson Thursday night, and he said he talked it over with his wife, and he's going to coach. Grace also wants to help out, so we might have her sell tickets or candy, or maybe she could be an assistant coach too.

The sleepover was so much fun. We did everything I told you we were going to do and more. And we didn't get a whole lot of sleep, which drove Olivia's mom crazy because we kept waking her up.

Dr. Matt never woke up, though. Olivia says he sleeps like the dead. Reminds me of Kayla. I think a tornado could hit our trailer and send it halfway across town, and she wouldn't even wake up.

And you know what? It turns out that I kind of like Zoe. Crazy, right? But I guess if we're both going to be friends with Olivia, then we'll need to be friends with each other too.

I'm afraid Jacob might get jealous that Olivia and I are friends again, which could mean I don't spend as much time with him. But I'll just have to make sure that doesn't happen.

I don't want him to think I ditched him for Olivia the way Olivia ditched me for Zoe. I know what that feels like, and it's not fun. It's not exactly the same, because Jacob and I are still as good of friends as we ever were. But it's hard when your best friend starts hanging out with someone else. He has other friends too, so that's good, but I want us to always be friends.

Mom's calling me to dinner, so I'll sign off now.

Love,
Mustang Macy

SUNDAY
October 15

Dear Miss W,

You have made my year. And that is *not* an exaggeration. I was sitting at lunch at church today, and I was distracted because Kinzie was being the ultimate three-year-old and driving me absolutely crazy. But I wasn't too distracted to hear something very interesting in a conversation between your mom and Mrs. Monroe.

They were talking about how you've decided to stay in Hanley after this year! *Whoop! Whoop! Whoop!* I just got up and did a little happy dance. Tanner rolled his eyes at me, but I don't care, because I am soooo elated!

Yes, I realize that I will only have you as a teacher for one year, so as far as that goes, it didn't matter if you stayed here or went back to St. Louis. But I see you at church, and you've started picking us up every week, even if it's not raining. And I'll see you around town. And maybe when I'm in high school, you'll be my basketball coach.

By the time I heard that news, you had already left church, so I didn't get to talk to you. But I can't wait to see you at school tomorrow so I can tell you how ecstatic I am about you staying here.

I don't think you even knew that I knew you were planning to leave us at the end of the school year, but I don't care. I'm going to tell you anyway!

Good night, Miss W. You're my favorite!

Love,
Mustang Macy

MUSTANG

JESSIE

If you enjoyed this book, tell your mom, aunt, grandma, teacher, or other adult friend she should read *Mustang Macy*'s companion novel: *Mustang Jessie*.

The companion novel has the same characters, setting, and timeline as this book, but it's written from Miss W's point of view. After your novel companion reads her book, the two of you can discuss the novels together.

Ask a parent or other trusted adult to help you find discussion questions and more information about our characters and books on our website.

anovelcompanion.com

ACKNOWLEDGMENTS

Mom and Dad, I can't thank you enough for always believing in me, supporting me, and being examples of people who live well and serve others. Without you, A Novel Companion would not exist.

Thank you to Claire and Maura for being my first readers and giving invaluable feedback on the content and characters. Thanks also to Maura for proofreading the book. Nicholas and Vera, your turn is coming once you get a little older!

My team of beta readers, proofreaders, experts, cheerleaders, and general advice-givers has been invaluable throughout the entire process of creating *Mustang Jessie* and *Mustang Macy*. Thanks to Claire, Maura, Karen Klebe, Jennifer Lyell, Holley Maher, Kate Massot, Laura Lee Rose, Amy Simpson, Jenny Spiers, Lisa Styles, Ryanne Tilley, Jenn Whitmer, and Beth Wilkerson.

I am also extremely grateful for my designer, Megan Weitzel, who did an amazing job creating the characters, book covers, and logo.

Thanks also to my brother, Chad, and the Baugh & Dunn crew for your support and encouragement.

Above all, I am grateful to God for giving me the idea for A Novel Companion and providing the talents, ability, and partners to carry it out.

ABOUT THE AUTHOR

For more than a decade, Dana Wilkerson has written and edited countless magazine articles, Sunday school lessons, and non-fiction trade books. She is the collaborative writer of four books, two of which have been *New York Times* best sellers: *The Vow: The True Events That Inspired the Movie* (Kim and Krickitt Carpenter) and *Balancing It All* (Candace Cameron Bure).

She created A Novel Companion in the summer of 2017, and she hopes millions will be inspired to live well and serve others as a result of reading her books. *Mustang Macy* and *Mustang Jessie* are her first companion novels.

Dana lives in Missouri and enjoys traveling, reading, visiting her nieces and nephew, and attending St. Louis Cardinals games.

Made in the USA
San Bernardino, CA
24 November 2017